With thanks to Kate Weller! **J.H.**

For Rosina **P.C.**

First published 1998 by Walker Books Ltd
87 Vauxhall Walk, London SE11 5HJ

10 9 8 7 6 5 4 3 2 1

Text © 1998 Judy Hindley
Illustrations © 1998 Pat Casey

This book has been typeset in AT Arta

Printed in Hong Kong

British Library Cataloguing in Publication Data
A catalogue record for this book is
available from the British Library.

ISBN 0-7445-6085-3

THE BEST THING ABOUT A PUPPY

WALKER BOOKS
AND SUBSIDIARIES
LONDON • BOSTON • SYDNEY

Judy Hindley

illustrated by Patricia Casey

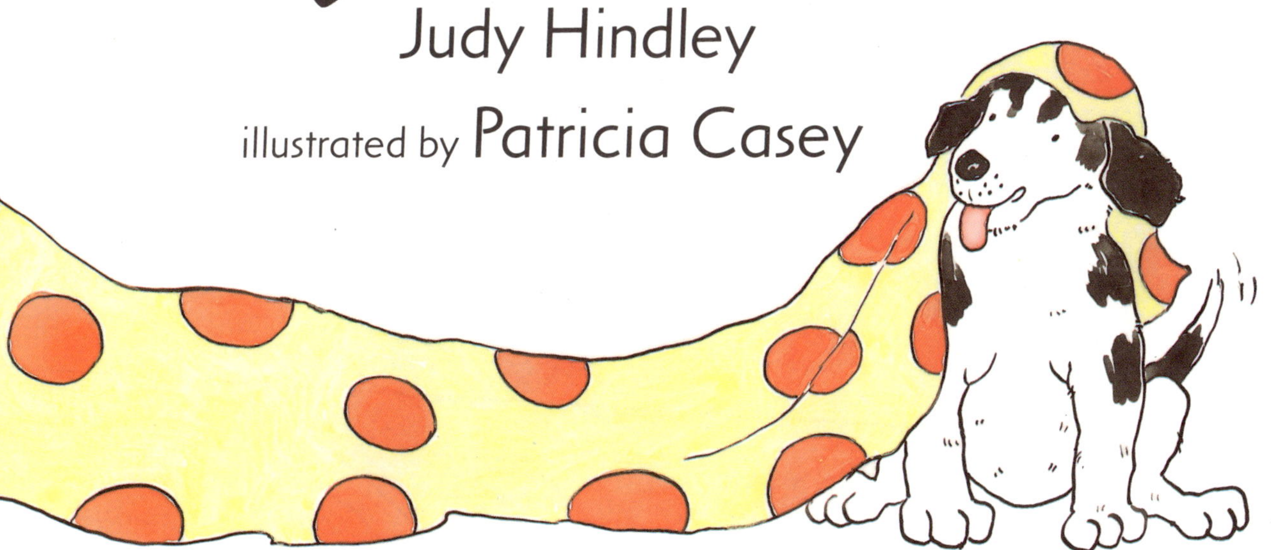

The good
thing about a
puppy is,
he's warm
and
wriggly.

The bad thing is,
he won't
keep still.

The good thing is,
the way he
rolls and
bounces.

The bad thing is,
he goes and jumps
in puddles – and that's
just when he bounces back,
and shakes himself and
wants a cuddle.

The good thing is,

you get to walk him every day.

The bad thing is,

he wants to go his own way.

The good thing is, he loves to chase a ball.
The bad thing is,
he hates to give it back.

The good thing is,
he likes to race
with you.

The bad thing is,

he trips you up!

The good thing is,
he knows just when
to comfort you.